P9-CFU-640

THIS BOOK BELONGS TO

Emma Jaye

Good People Everywhere

Lynea Gillen
Illustrated by Kristina Swarner

Three Pebble Press, LLC
Portland, Oregon

Good People Everywhere

By Lynea Gillen

Copyright © 2012 by Three Pebble Press, LLC

Illustration Copyright © 2012 by Kristina Swarner

All rights reserved.

No part of this book may be reproduced in any form
without written permission of the copyright owners.

Printed in USA

ISBN: 978-0-9799289-8-7
ISBN: 978-0-9799289-9-4 (ebook)

Three Pebble Press, LLC
10040 SW 25th Ave
Portland, OR 97219-6325 U.S.A.

ThreePebblePress.com

Volume discounts available.

Layout Design by paisleyarts.com

Ninth Printing 2017

Gillen, Lynea.
  Good people everywhere / Lynea Gillen ; illustrated by Kristina Swarner.

  p. : col. ill. ; cm.

  Content: A story to help children become mindful of caring people in
their world, to ease their fears and to develop their sense of gratitude.
Includes two activity pages to encourage children to find the good people
in their lives.
  Interest age group: 003-008.
  Issued also as an ebook.
  ISBN: 978-0-9799289-8-7

  1. Kindness—Juvenile fiction. 2. Gratitude—Juvenile fiction.
3. Interpersonal relations—Juvenile fiction. 4. Kindness—Fiction.
5. Gratitude—Fiction. 6. Interpersonal relations—Fiction. I. Swarner,
Kristina. II. Title.

PZ7.G55 Goo 2012
[Fic]   2012938321

To my sister, Paula.

Today,
in neighborhoods
all over the world,
millions and millions
of people are doing
very good things.

Today, carpenters are building
fences and houses, and repairing homes
that have been damaged by storms.

Today, moms and dads are cooking dinners for their families,

and cooks are working in kitchens
making meals for people
who don't have homes.

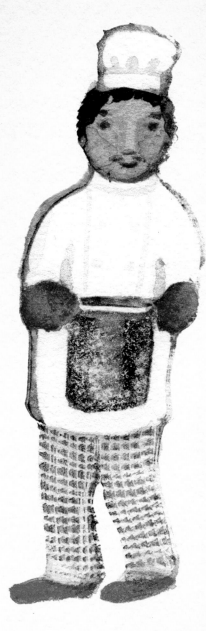

Doctors and midwives are
delivering babies and
gently passing them
into the eager arms of their parents.

Teachers are teaching math,
spelling and reading skills,

musicians are opening their hearts
and playing beautiful music,

and dancers are leaping across
dance floors, practicing performances
that will bring joy to their friends,
their families and their communities.

Today, people are planting seeds,

picking fruits and vegetables,

and driving them
to grocery stores all around the
world, so you can have
a ripe, juicy orange in your lunch.

Today, a child is trying
her very best to do well
on her science test,

and a teenage boy is helping
a young child who is sad and lonely.

Today, a first grade boy is helping
a friend who has a skinned knee,

and a big sister is holding her baby brother
while her mother runs across the street
to help a neighbor.

Today, millions and millions of people
will do very good things.

And so will you.

I wonder what you will do?

Who are the good people in your community?

Close your eyes and think of all the good people in your life. Think of your friends, families, neighbors and teachers. Now, think of other people who help you, like store clerks, the mail carrier, and the farmers who grow the food you eat. Draw a circle with these people around it like the drawing here. You can draw paper dolls, stick figures or faces. Draw yourself in the center. Write down the names of the people around and inside the circle. Decorate your circle and put it in a special place to help you remember the good people in your life.

Create a "Good Person" Award

Have you ever had someone thank you for something good you have done? Didn't that feel good? You can make someone else feel good by giving them a good person award. Draw an award like the one on this page, or make up a style of your own. Write a thank you note inside the award. Decorate it and give it to the person. Then watch them smile!

Lynea Gillen, LPC, has been sharing her love of literature with children for over 30 years as a school teacher and counselor. Now in private practice, she is the creator of the highly regarded Mindful Moments Cards, as well as two Mom's Choice Award winners: the book *Yoga Calm for Children* and DVD *Kids Teach Yoga: Flying Eagle*. Lynea lives in Portland, Oregon, with her husband Jim, where she enjoys hiking, gardening and spending time with all the good people in her life.

Kristina Swarner is an award-winning illustrator (Sydney Taylor Book Award) whose numerous books include *Before You Were Born* and *Enchanted Lions*. Using imagery and inspiration from memories of exploring old houses, woods and gardens as a child, her work is often described as "magical" and "dreamlike." When not painting, Kristina enjoys music, reading and trying to grow trees on her balcony. She lives in Chicago.

Share your stories at: **GoodPeopleEverywhere.com**
Facebook.com/GoodPeopleEverywhere

Other Family and School Resources from Lynea Gillen

Little Banty Chicken and the Big Dream
An enchanting tale of one little chicken with the courage to make her dream come true with the support of the moon and her barnyard friends.

Yoga Calm for Children: Educating Heart, Mind and Body
Help children develop self-control, attention, fitness and social/emotional skills with this award-winning handbook.

Mindful Moments Car
Short contemplations that develop imaginatio attention, relaxation skil and positive feelings.

Order these and other products at ThreePebblePress.com.